Happy Valentine's Day
Owen! ♡
Love always,
    Mommy & Daddy

How Deep is the Sea?

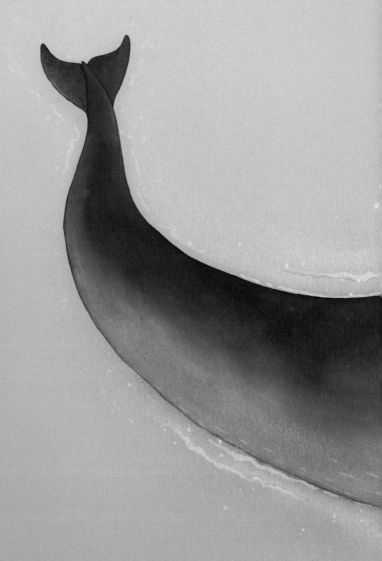

Edited by Gillian Doherty
Digital manipulation by John Russell
With thanks to Dr. Margaret and Dr. John Rostron for information about the sea

First published in 2009 by Usborne Publishing Ltd, 83-85 Saffron Hill, London ECIN 8RT, England.
www.usborne.com Copyright © 2009 Usborne Publishing Ltd.

How Deep is the Sea?

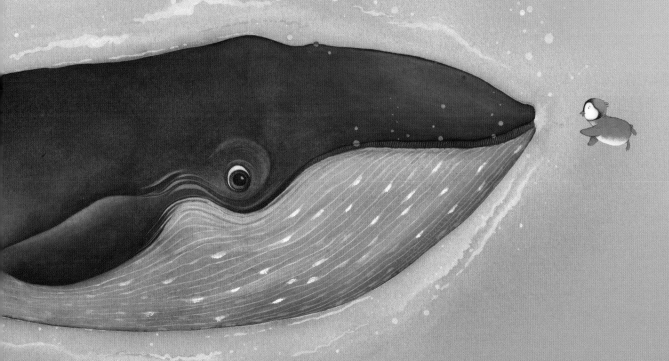

Anna Milbourne

Illustrated by Serena Riglietti

Designed by Laura Wood

Pipkin was a very small penguin
who was always asking
very big questions.

How big was a dinosaur?

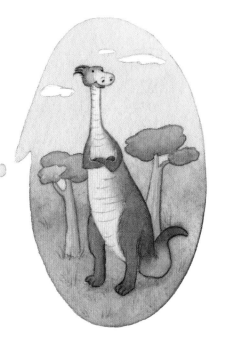

Does chocolate
grow on trees?

What makes snow
fall from the sky?

But the thing he wanted to know most of all was...

"How deep
is the sea?"

"Penguins are really good swimmers," said his Mama.
"Why don't you go and have a look?"

Pipkin took a very deep breath
and dived into the sea.

He swam down a little way into the sparkling blue
and found a seal catching silver fish.

"Excuse me," said Pipkin.
"How deep is the sea?"

"Deep enough to hold more fish
than I could ever eat," said the seal.
"Would you like to stay for lunch?"

"Sorry, I can't stop now," said Pipkin.
"I'm off to find the bottom of the sea."

He swam down a little further into the deepening blue
and found the biggest creature he'd ever seen
singing a rumbly song.

"Excuse me," said Pipkin.
"How deep is the sea?"

"Deeper than a big blue whale like
ME has ever been," said the creature.
"Would you like to stay and sing to my
blue whale friends across the sea?"

"Sorry, I can't stop now," said Pipkin,
"I'm off to find the bottom of the sea."

Pipkin swam down a little further into the darkening blue,
and found a salty sea dog in a yellow submarine.

"Excuse me," said Pipkin.
"How deep is the sea?"

"Deep enough to need a submarine to reach the very bottom," said the salty sea dog. "I'm going there now. Would you like to join me?"

"Yes please," said Pipkin.

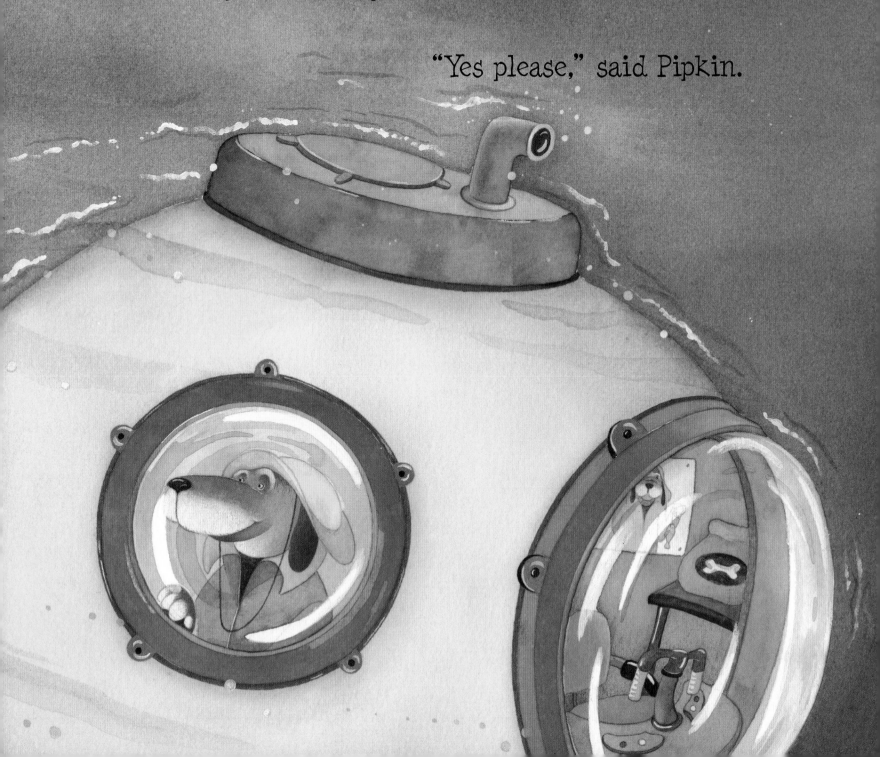

The submarine took them down...

...and down...

...and down...

...to where the sea turned night-black
and there was no one else around.

Then, one by one,
twinkling lights began to appear.

All kinds of wonderful, lit-up creatures were swimming around in the dark.

"Excuse me," said Pipkin.
"How deep is the sea?"

"Deep enough to have whole mountains at the bottom,"
said one of the twinkly creatures. "Look."

And sure enough, just below,
was a range of towering mountains...

"Is this the very deepest part?"
asked Pipkin.

"Not quite," said the twinkly creature, and it pointed to a valley. "Down there is the very deepest part of the sea."

So the yellow submarine took them down into the valley.

It was very deep

and very dark

and very,

very

quiet.

Flump went the submarine
as it landed on the bottom.

"I wonder whether anything lives
all the way down here?" whispered Pipkin.

They peered into the darkness,
but nothing came to say hello.
So they sat for a while at the bottom of the sea
with miles and miles of water above them.

"Ready to go home?" asked the salty sea dog.
"Yes please," said Pipkin.

The yellow submarine took
them all the way back up
to the top of the sea.

Pipkin said to his Mama:

"The sea is very, VERY deep.
It's deep enough to hold more fish than a seal can ever eat,
and deeper than a big blue whale has ever been,
and deep enough to have whole mountains at the bottom,
and lots of twinkly creatures hardly anyone's ever seen."

"And it's deep enough for very small penguins to have very big adventures," said his Mama as she rubbed him dry.

"I'm proud of you, my little Pip."

Come this way to see how deep Pipkin went.

Open the envelope to see how deep Pipkin went.